Dragons in Winter
Chapbook Anthology

Edited by B. Heather Mantler

TABLE OF CONTENTS

In Which I Summon a Dragon
Sarah Dahlmann

"DRAGONS AREN'T REAL!" They scream at me from the sidewalk. Half a dozen of them, standing there, bare hands stuffed into pockets, shivering in light jackets, jeans, and running shoes. Too "cool", I guess, to dress appropriately for our cold and deeply snowy weather.

I ignore them and keep working.

Already I have eight snowballs, each as tall as me, lined up more or less in a row. I pack snow in and around them to form a long, sinuous body. Next I add a carefully tapering tail, barbed at the end, and wings laid back along the sides of the body. Then a ridge of spikes down the middle of the back, followed by fore and hind limbs with clawed toes. I mould scales all the way from tail to head.

The details of the head take longer and much more careful sculpting. The brow with a pair of curved horns. Giant, heavy lidded eyes. Tooth filled snout. Lines of whiskers drawn carefully back along the face.

I'm too focused on the work to be cold. Too engaged to notice when those on the sidewalk grow bored and walk away, laughing among themselves.

At last the sculpture is good enough. I dig the scrap of paper from my pocket. Unfolding it, I smooth out the creases and crinkles. The symbol is as clear as when I copied it from the huge, old, leatherbound tome Grandfather keeps hidden in his study. He's allowed me to read it, a few pages at a time, under his strict supervision. Now, painstakingly, I copy the symbol onto the brow of my snow dragon.

Then it's done and I step back to survey my handiwork. It's impressive, if I do say so myself.

1

"Hey! Kid!"

Frowning, I turn toward the street to see a man holding a professional looking camera. He's waving enthusiastically.

"That's awesome work! Did you do it all by yourself?"

"Yessir!" I can't help a proud grin.

"Would you mind if I take some pictures of it? For a local interest piece."

"Sure." I stuff the scrap of paper into my pocket. Then I step back, away from the snow sculpture.

"Ed Trake, photographer," He walks across the much trampled snow of the open field to hand me a business card for the small local free paper. He has a laminated press ID on a cord around his neck which says the same thing.

"My editor will love this." He adds as he holds up the camera and begins taking shots. He circles around to capture the dragon from all angles, "How long did this take you?"

I glance at the sky which is beginning to darken, "All afternoon."

"Just today?" Ed's surprise is clear, "Fast work for something this big."

I shrug it off. When I'm focused on a project, I lose time and nothing distracts me.

He takes one more picture and gives me a smile, "Thank you. This really is awesome work." Then he's gone and I have to run. The sky is nearing full dark and Grandmother is a stickler for punctuality, especially for meals.

ALL THROUGH SUPPER, for which I was just on time, I can feel Grandfather's eyes on me. But he doesn't say a word until after, when we can meet in his study while Grandmother sets her kitchen in her preferred order.

Grandfather's study is a place of wonder. One wall lined with floor to ceiling bookshelves full of beautiful old books. The opposite wall also covered in shelves, but for displaying a wide variety of everything but books. My favourite is a carving of a golden dragon very similar in appearance to the one I sculpted of snow today. A third wall taken up mostly by a window now hidden behind heavy floor to ceiling curtains. His desk rests beside the door, paired with a comfortable big leather chair. The center of the floor is taken up by a low square table surrounded by large, thick cushions.

Now, I settle on a cushion and Grandfather into his desk chair, which he turns to face me.

"So you tried it?"

I shrug, "I sculpted a snow dragon. Good enough there might be pictures in the free paper."

Grandfather smiles a little sadly, "It is what it is. No more, no less."

"Did I do something wrong?" I watch him carefully for any sign of an answer, good or bad. But his face is impossible to read.

"Go get some sleep," He instructs, "Check on it in the morning."

BY THE TIME GRANDMOTHER is done with me and needing my help around the house, it's afternoon. I escape the house as soon as I can and run back to the field, slipping and sliding in the small mound of new snow which had fallen overnight. But, when I arrive at the field, there's no sculpture anywhere to be seen. Only a much trampled expanse of snow, almost as if someone or something had come in the night and carried it off. I don't see any evidence of it having been destroyed. Although, had those harassing me about it yesterday seen the final result, they would no doubt have attempted to do so. Still, no matter what happened, the sculpture is gone.

My shoulders slump as I turn back towards home, now trudging through the snow. All that work yesterday for nothing. My eyes focus on where my feet are going, not looking up or around, my hands stuffed into my pockets.

A second later, I'm soaring through the air, talons clenched around my shoulders, digging in painfully. The neighbourhood falls away below me, everything shrinking to doll house size in a moment.

I can't scream. I can't breathe. I can't close my eyes and not see the dizzying, expanding distance between my feet and the ground.

Then I'm surrounded by cloud, moisture soaking through all my layers of clothing and winter gear. I can't see anything below me now. I feel like I'm choking, suffocating. There's no air up this high.

An upward surge and a glimpse of bright sun on white before everything goes dark.

"...TOLD YOU TO TRANSPORT the human another way." The voice reminds me of Grandmother except it's too raspy, "They can't breathe without that soupy gunk they call air."

"There wasn't room to land," A defensive voice, much lower and gravelly, but competely unfamiliar, "And besides, that soupy gunk, as you call it, was burning my lungs out. I had to get high. Also, I brought the human alive. Maybe this one will serve."

"You'd better hope so. If her majesty isn't found soon, none of us will be breathing anything."

I can breathe again, although the air tastes funny and my head spins. But when I shift position the tiniest bit, my shoulders scream in pain and I groan audibly.

"The human's awake." The first voice turns dry, "And far from fully healed yet."

"I didn't mean to damage it," The second voice sulks, "Can't you heal it faster?"

"No, I can't. Healing takes time. And humans aren't its. They have names just the same as we do."

I open my eyes, a crack at a time, to find myself tucked into a tiny niche in a much larger space. In the dim light, it's hard to tell what the walls and ceiling are constructed of.

There really isn't much to see at all. I'm lying on something soft, at least. I'm having a hard time telling what.

But, out in the larger space, I can see two dragons. And I know they're dragons because they're nearly identical to my snow sculpture, although one is crimson and the other indigo. Their scales shine as if lit from within. Both are currently looking straight at me and I can't help shivering.

"Do not move," Evidently the first voice belongs to the crimson dragon, "Your shoulders were deeply cut," A glare at the indigo dragon, "And could reopen still."

I swallow hard.

"We will find you something to eat and drink, but you must rest and recover."

DAYS LATER, I'm certain my grandparents must be frantic, but I'm finally healed enough to move around. And I'm as curious as ever about that first overheard conversation between the dragons caring for me. Now, the pair of them return with food for me. Both look as grave and solemn as dragons can.

"It is odd, young human," The crimson dragon passes me the food, "Your summoning a dragon now, of all times."

I frown as I begin eating. Why the timing would matter, I have no idea.

"Long ago," The crimson dragon settles back, serpentine eyes on me, "Our queen was taken from us." A pause, "I suppose that means nothing to a human. Our queen is most powerful, able to rule over all dragons as well as protect your world from... well, you would never sleep again if you knew the forces arrayed against you."

"And without her?" I can't help a shudder.

"The rest of us can maintain enough protection. Or we have been able to up until now. But we are battered, weary, losing strength and will to continue. If our queen is not found quickly..."

Shivering, I nod to myself, my food forgotten, "Why involve a human?"

"Our queen is somewhere in your world. And your world is a place we cannot go. At least not for more than a moment. Worse, she is not herself, so far as we can see."

"So she'll be hard to find?"

"Were she easy to find, we would have long ago. While we know what she looked like as our queen, we have no idea what her current form is."

"We have images of her," The indigo dragon speaks up, "Whether they would aid or hinder you in a search."

"I think," Recalling my food and need to heal, I take a bite and chew it slowly while I consider the issue, "I would be able to return to my home after?"

"We only need you to find her location for us. We ought to be able to resolve our issues once we know where she is."

"I think... I want to see the images of her you have. Maybe it will help more than you think."

"After you eat." The crimson dragon responds.

AFTER I FINISH MY FOOD, the crimson dragon uses extreme care to pick me up and set me on the back of the indigo dragon. I cling tight to the spikes on the back as they lumber along to a wall covered in a gigantic mural. The centerpiece of the whole work is a golden dragon which I immediately recognize. I would know that dragon anywhere.

"I know where your queen is."

"Already, from only this?" The crimson dragon sounds sceptical.

"This image is identical to a carving of a dragon in my grandfather's collection of knick knacks. You said she'd been given a form you didn't know and haven't been able to find. A carving kind of makes sense."

"You would retrieve this carving for us?" The crimson dragon looks hopeful.

"Shouldn't be hard. But I need to get home."

"Then I will send you, but by a means safer for both you

and us. Get this carving and leave it where you made the summons."

"I'll do that."

AND SO I FIND myself standing back in the field where I had sculpted the snow dragon. Everything looks exactly as it had when I last left, which causes me to frown. My shoulders are still healing and tender.

Knowing the dragon carving will still be in Grandfather's study, I set out for home, fully expecting to be in all kinds of trouble for being away as long as I have.

However, when I enter the house it is quiet and everything looks the same as I recall from when I went out. In fact, I find Grandmother still at the task I'd left her dealing with. A glance at the calendar on the kitchen wall, which shows a page a day, tells me either my grandparents have forgotten to change it or it's still the same day I left.

I shiver, but hurry to Grandfather's study in search of the golden dragon carving.

"You've been injured."

I whirl to see Grandfather seated in his desk chair, his gaze on me critical and assessing.

"How?"

Rather than attempt an unbelieveable sounding explanation, I show him my shoulders and the healing talon marks.

Slowly, he nods to himself, "Still they seek the one they believe to be their queen?"

I swallow hard, but nod. How could he possibly know?

He seems to sense my question. His expression turns sad and he sighs tiredly.

"Perhaps, to the dragons, the queen is what they claim. Our ancestors record a very different version of events. What happened and why the dragon queen was transformed." He reaches for a book resting on the desk. This isn't the dragon book he keeps hidden. This is a much smaller book, looking

7

more like someone's journal. He holds it out to me and I take it.

"Time, to the dragons, is little like what we experience. You have time to read this. And time to make a decision."

Swallowing hard, I nod. Then I take the book to my bedroom and settle in to read.

I KNOW WHAT I HAVE TO DO.

I start by returning the journal to Grandfather's study. This time he isn't there. I leave the journal on his desk and take the dragon carving from the shelf. While I know it had taken me some time to read the entire journal from beginning to end, I find it disturbing to pass through an empty house. There's no sign of either of my grandparents anywhere. Outside, I turn my footsteps towards the open field. As I walk, snow falls, adding to what has already freshly fallen on the ground. Hopefully it will be enough. The dragon carving is surprisingly warm in my pocket. The field is empty, coated with newly fallen snow. I set to work making gigantic snowballs.

My snow sculpting totally absorbs my attention as I work. This second one is much more detailed than the first, taking far longer to complete each part. When I get to the head, I carefully pack the dragon carving into the middle of the snowball. Then I set to work finishing the head as the last part.

Once I'm finally happy with my work, I step back and circle around to survey it from all angles. My snow dragon looks as good as I think it ever will. Now I reach into my pocket and retrieve a crumpled scrap of paper. The symbol on it is still visible enough for me to copy it onto the brow of the snow dragon.

But this time, as I finish, the paper begins to smoke and flame appears to lick the corners. I drop it, watching it burst into full flame and curl up into ash long before it hits the ground. I shiver, stepping back.

The ground trembles beneath my feet and bright light flares from the snow sculpture. I have to cover my eyes until it fades away. When I can see again, I take another step back, shivering involuntarily, before I manage to draw a breath and compose myself.

"Who dares summon the Queen of Dragons?!" The words shake the ground.

"One who knows the Queen has much to set right," Now I step forward, raising my voice defiantly, "One know knows that to summon the Queen is to bind the Queen to her proper tasks. One who will remember to summon the Queen each year to keep her bound to those tasks for the safety of dragons and humans alike. Go forth and set the Queen's domain in order."

A roar of anger and frustration rocks the world around me, followed by stomping of giant feet. But, rage as she might, the Queen of Dragons cannot harm any while properly bound to the tasks of her office. Eventually, she settles down and vanishes, leaving me standing in the falling snow. I pick up the dragon carving which has fallen into the snow in her passage and tuck it into my pocket before walking home.

GRANDFATHER IS WAITING for me when I enter his study to return the carving to its place on the shelf. I can feel his eyes on me as I do that and then turn to face him.

"So we have a proper summoner in the family once more?" He isn't at all upset.

"Why haven't we until now?" I settle onto a cushion below his chair.

"Dragons aren't the only ones who forget the whole truth of matters," Grandfather smiles fondly, "You have done well. Now, look at this." He holds out a newspaper and I take it.

It's the most recent edition of the free paper. The pictures of my original snow sculpture are front and center, on the front page, along with a short caption.

The Thrill of the Hunt
Jennie Evans

FIVE. THE LARGE BEAST STOOD near the edge of the meadow, hesitant as to whether or not it would risk the open area. *Four.* From this distance, it appeared almost docile as it carefully placed each paw down into the deep snow, frosty breath escaping its snout as it exhaled. Malakai wasn't fooled though; he knew the ursine monster was more than willing to kill even the strongest of people and was well-equipped for the job. The beast's massive paws and thick, sharp claws—easily capable of shredding flesh and crushing armour—were tinged a rusty brown. It wasn't hard to guess where the colouration came from.

Three. It was the entire reason he even had a job in the first place. The locals called it a *jabör*, which loosely translated to "giant bear" in their native tongue. The *jabör* had been causing trouble by attacking anyone who set foot outside the village, which was worrisome as many of the children liked to play in the surrounding forest. He had been asked, in no uncertain terms, to kill the beast. With the promise of money, Malakai had been more than happy to accept.

Crouched at the opposite edge of the meadow, his lithe dragonoid frame was easy to conceal amidst the snowy undergrowth. His skin—a light sandy colour—blended in surprisingly well with the soft snow. His long, reptilian tail twitched in anticipation. *Two.* He exhaled, steadying his hands. In the corner of his vision, he saw the bright red bolt of his crossbow, ready to fire. *One.* A small grin tugged at the corners of his mouth.

Zero. With a soft *thwunk*, the bolt shot toward the *jabör* and buried itself in its skull. The beast wavered for several seconds and let out a mournful cry before dropping to the ground, dead. Malakai stood up and let out his breath in a white puff of steam. It was another job done. He retrieved the bolt and took one last look at the monster. A thin layer of snow was already beginning to dust its fur. Crimson splatters speckled the snow around its head, the only colour in the otherwise drab landscape.

"WE ARE ETERNALLY GRATEFUL for your help, traveler," the village chief gushed, his head bowed in thanks. Malakai leaned against the wall and feigned indifference by checking his short claws. In the background, a hearty fire crackled, bathing the room in a comfortable orange glow.

"The best gratitude you can give me is the money you promised. That's all I need," Malakai answered curtly. The chief looked slightly taken aback but disappeared quickly into another room. Malakai tapped his foot restlessly, his gaze fixed out the window into the snowy world beyond. All the waiting in between hunts made him impatient. He longed for the thrill of the hunt, the cathartic silence of nature, and the quick demise that was sure to meet his targets. He was a bounty hunter, and he lived and breathed his job.

The chief returned and handed him a satchel of money. He peeked inside; gold coins stared back at him. It didn't look like any were amiss, though he sighed inwardly at how little there was in the bag. That was the problem with finding work in a small town, he supposed.

"There you go, traveler. Thank you again for your service to the village," the chief concluded with a nod. Malakai started toward the door and then paused.

"You wouldn't happen to know anyone else who would need my assistance, would you?" It was less of a question and more of a demand.

"Well erm…" the chief stuttered and cleared his throat. "Not around here, no. But if you travel north to Lunashire, they might have some work for you. They are a larger town, after all," he explained, nodding affirmatively at the suggestion.

"Perhaps I'll pay them a visit," Malaki mused, a half-grin lighting up his face as he walked outside. Lunashire it was, then.

LUNASHIRE WAS A LARGER TOWN, but that didn't make it any more impressive. Malakai scrunched up his snout as he passed quaint houses with grimy windows and sagging roofs. Fires glowed in each, casting an orange light in contrast to the cold blue tones of the roads and snow. Dusk was already starting to fall, and he had yet to find another bounty. The villagers seemed to live dull, oblivious lives and were of no help to him. He regretted making the trip up here.

As darkness settled on the village, Malakai found his way to an inn. A small bell chimed as he entered the lobby. The innkeeper was civil, but much like the others, didn't have any information to offer him. He took a room for the night. Sleep came quickly to him.

At the first few rays of light, Malakai awoke. He stretched and noticed with a quip of frustration that some of his muscles were sore. *I'm out of practice*, he thought to himself bitterly. The utter lack of things to hunt lately was throwing him off. He had to find a new bounty, and soon.

Grabbing a quick breakfast on his way out of the inn, he entered the streets to the faint glow of dawn. The snow twinkled, a thin layer of ice crusting its surface from the previous night's cold. The air was crisp. Not many others stirred in the sleepy village so early in the morning.

Malakai distractedly shifted the strap of his crossbow. He wandered to the outskirts of town. As he gazed into the frosty forests beyond, a sharp voice roused him from his trance.

"Malakai Verick? What an awful surprise to find you here,"

the voice intoned monotonously. Malakai spun quickly on his feet to face whoever it was. He was greeted with another dragonoid, about his size but with a sturdier build and darker skin. Vivid turquoise eyes bore into him with contempt. Malakai sighed as he recognized the figure.

"Jett," he replied monosyllabically. He wasn't very fond of the man. Although the two may have been friends a lifetime ago, their ideals had torn them apart as they grew older. It had been years since they had last seen each other, and for Malakai, even that was too soon.

"Pleasant as ever, aren't you Malakai? Looks like you're out playing with your forest friends again," Jett gestured to the crossbow slung across Malakai's back, glinting in the morning light. Jett always had a way of sounding snide with whatever he said. Malakai snarled back.

"Don't bother wasting my time," Malakai growled, pushing past Jett to return to town. The latter was silent for a moment.

"Then...I guess you aren't interested in hunting the monster I found," Jett lowered his voice, shrugged, and started to walk away. Malakai stopped, and inwardly cursed himself for doing so. Jett could easily be lying, and would make the bounty hunter nearly beg for the information, but if it was a lead...

"Just tell me where it is," Malakai conceded, hoping the other dragonoid wouldn't give him too much trouble. Jett's smile widened and his eyes sparkled mischievously.

"That's the Malakai I know. Always up for an adventure."

AS MALAKAI TRUDGED through deep snow, he started to wonder if Jett had played a trick on him. There was nothing in this frozen chunk of land. A strong gust of wind buffeted him, causing him to stop for a second to catch his breath. The weather was vicious and the land inhospitable. How could any sort of large monster live in such an unforgiving landscape? He cursed it all.

Needing to rest for a minute, he made his way over to a rock face that protected him from most of the wind. Plopping down to the ground, he exhaled heavily, resting his head against the rock behind him. The wind howled around him, snow swirled chaotically, and all he could see was white, white, and more white. Except for that blob of grey in the distance. Wait.

Malakai brought his head forward and squinted to try and make out the grey patch better. It was impossible to tell what it was, or if it was simply a trick of his imagination. The snowstorm didn't help visibility at all. He observed it intently for a few minutes, but it didn't seem to move or disappear. Hauling himself up and brushing snow off his shoulders and legs, he fixed his gaze on the grey and started out toward it.

He was relieved to find that he was, indeed, getting closer to it. As he drew nearer, the details began to form into the shape of trees. Somehow, despite the raging snowstorm, an entire mini forest grew. It was only when he stood next to one of the trees that he realized why. Half-obscured by heavy clouds, a cliff face loomed over the trees, protecting them from most of the elements.

As he stepped foot into the grove, the wind died down to a low whistle. The silence was almost oppressive. He became acutely aware of his own breathing, his slightest movements, and the gentle swaying of the trees and their branches. Snow drifted down from the canopy above, and every once in a while, a cluster of snow would fall off a branch with a soft *whump* as it hit the ground below.

He pressed further into the small forest until he came to a short cliff wall. Only a couple of metres tall, he scaled it without a problem. The trees had thinned out atop the ledge, and before he had taken another step, his senses buzzed. He had the distinct feeling he wasn't alone anymore.

A more thorough survey confirmed his suspicions. Not twenty metres away lay a very large grey form. He almost hadn't noticed it at first since it was close in colour to the surrounding grey trees.

It was a dragon. Or, rather, it was *the* dragon: the one Jett had told him about. People called it Lion, named for its noble stature and raw power. Beyond that, the comparison held no similarity. Easily over five metres in length, it had no tail, no fur, not even any ears. Its body was long and thick, tapering to a sturdy neck and an elongated face and snout. It had six limbs, two of which were eerily humanoid. Its underbelly was the colour of the night sky, but otherwise, the creature held almost no colour. Its eyes, sixteen circular openings on its face, shimmered faintly with the colours of the rainbow. It had no pupils nor irises.

It hadn't noticed Malakai. The latter quickly crouched down into some bushes and pulled out his crossbow, loading a bolt. The dragon seemed content to amble slowly between the trees, pausing every few steps to swing its head around, almost as if it were observing the forest. Malakai's heart hammered in his chest, adrenaline coursing through his veins. He lined up his sights with the beast's head, smirked, and fired.

Near-silence permeated the forest as the bolt lanced through the air and struck the monster in the head. It let out an otherworldly surprised shriek and reeled in shock. Staggering, it righted itself and swung around to face Malakai's hiding spot. For a split second, the two faced each other, neither one daring to move nor look away. Then, the creature grabbed the embedded crossbow bolt and ripped it out, flinging it away with anger. It looked unfazed but enraged. Its eyes rippled red. Malakai's smile faded.

As he went to load another crossbow bolt, a flash of blue illuminated his vision before a loud explosion burst around him. The sound of splintering trees assaulted his senses as he tumbled across the ground, disoriented. Before he had time to recover, the dragon had leaped toward him at lightning speed and lifted him off the ground with terrifying strength. Its head came mere centimetres away from his own as it stared deeply at him. After several tense seconds, the dragon lowered him to the ground with surprising gentleness and took off into the forest.

Malakai wasn't about to give up. Shaking his head to clear his mind, he bounded off through the forest in pursuit of the monster. Branches whipped past him as he weaved through trees, snow flying in all directions. He paused after a few minutes, panting. A small gust of wind ruffled the branches and his clothes, but otherwise, it was quiet.

A split second before impact, he leaped aside as another flash of blue hurtled past him and exploded into the trees and underbrush. Moments later, Lion crashed through the trees and went straight for Malakai with another screech. He rolled out of the way and swiftly loaded his crossbow. As the dragon turned to face him, Malakai shot the bolt into its neck, spurning another cry from the beast. Taking advantage of stunning it, he fumbled to load the crossbow anew and fire another shot. This one stuck into its side. It stumbled, hitting its shoulder against a tree and sending a spray of snow into the air. Malakai managed a small smile as he felt the tide of battle turning to his favour. Or so he thought.

In the blink of an eye, the dragon disappeared and re-appeared behind him, pinning him to the ground with two thick arms. He twisted his head around to face his foe and struggled to try and grab his dagger from his side. Before he had a chance to, the creature formed a sphere of blue energy between its free hands. It looked at Malakai defiantly before pressing the sphere to his face. Everything went dark.

HE AWOKE GROGGILY. His mind felt heavy, as did his limbs. Groaning, he blinked a few times to try and wake himself up. Vision slowly came to him, blurry at first, but slowly sharpening into hues of brown and grey. He shut his eyes tightly for a moment, then opened them up wide. A room came into focus, and a familiar one at that. It was the inn room he had stayed at the night before. In Lunashire. He was back in town.

Malakai shifted his gaze to look around the room. His hunting equipment leaned against the wall, and his outdoor wear rested on a table. He got up shakily and sifted through the piles. Nothing seemed to be missing. After regaining a bit more composure and grabbing his gear, he headed to the innkeeper.

"Uh, hey," he began. *Smooth*, he thought to himself. Whatever had happened had shaken him more than he thought.

"Oh, good morning sir. How are you feeling today?" the innkeeper inquired. It was a good question. His thoughts and emotions were all over the place.

"Could be better, I guess," Malakai finally settled on an answer, shrugging. "What happened? For me to get here, I mean," he stumbled over his words. His head was stuffy and a headache had started to form. Words were not his allies right now.

"Someone brought you here last night. Said they found you at the edge of town, unconscious. You should be more careful about how hard you celebrate. Sleeping out in this weather, well…it's deadly." Was the innkeeper seriously lecturing him about drinking right now? He would've laughed if it didn't hurt his head so much. He settled for a small groan instead.

"Right…right," he mumbled. It would be easier to let the innkeeper think he was out drinking instead of…whatever happened. "Thanks." He inclined his head and left.

The stinging cold hit him immediately, clearing his mind of all thoughts and lingering grogginess. It was still morning, so at least he hadn't overslept, but more people were out wandering today. Some of them smiled as he passed but he wasn't inclined to return the gesture. Making his way to the quieter outskirts of town, he sat down and leaned against a stone wall, shutting his eyes.

Had he dreamed of the grove of trees and the monster? Maybe the cold had addled his brain and he had wandered back to town in a trance, which would explain how he ended up so close by. Something told him this wasn't the case, though. His chest ached from where the dragon had grabbed him, he was sure of it. So how did he end up on the outskirts of town after the encounter? He had no idea. He grunted in frustration. His headache was pounding, and he really didn't feel like thinking too hard right now.

Whatever happened, he was back in town and everything seemed to be normal. Tomorrow, he would find more bounties, more monsters to hunt. That was the nice thing about his job; there was always some sort of beast to fight. And, in the future, maybe he would come face-to-face with the mythical Lion again. With great effort, he hauled himself to his feet and shuffled back to the centre of town. From the nearby underbrush, several eyes glinted and then disappeared.

The Race of Farren
Frances Mantler

MICKLAND LISTENS TO THE STORY with a frown on his face but
no urgency, he is a middle-aged man, and the ways of people
rarely shock him anymore.

"Please help me, I went to my brother's house and the
door hung open. He, his wife and children are murdered in
their beds. Please, help me." A young man pleads with the
men gathered at Mickland's house as unending Serran winter
winds slam against building. Here the men of the settlement
gather since tilling the soil became unprofitable. The dirt and
seed scatter into the boulders where nothing grows.

"Mickland, what this settlement requires is a strong leader.
Celia is too busy healing to be an effective leader. You should
step forward," Hadrian presses.

"It takes more than a steady hand of a painter to rule Serran. If these Valen hear of such a declaration my death would
be the only result." Mickland shakes his head.

No one says anything until Hadrian speaks up again.

"They feared Nasserila. She told us what was needed."
Hadrian frowns. "We need to enforce Nasserila's laws."

"Hadrian, I am all for building a better life but I am not a
fighter. You need someone strong without fear," Mickland
answers.

"So, you are unwilling even as those killers chose their next
victim?" Hadrian asks with a frown on his face. "We have
sat here discussing this endlessly. Someone must stop these
murders if we are to survive here."

"I am a peaceful man. I need little and want to remain as I
am," Mickland says.

Another person says, but he checks out the window to see

that no Valen lurks nearby. "This devilish planet is punishing us for their evil ways."

Yet another says. "Another year of this and we shall all starve. Poor crops, attacks and murders, soon there will be only Valen left. Did we survive the rebellion on Dalsher's ship only to die at the hands of bureaucrats and scholars gone mad?"

Mickland frowns. "If it displeases you so much go and find some other place to settle. I will remain in this valley."

"And the circle goes around again. What will it take for you to act?" Hadrian frowns.

"Why must it be me? You come here and complain when is it time for you to act?" Mickland replies. "Why must it be me?"

There the conversation ends because they hear a noise outside. Mickland rises quickly and opens the door.

"Come inside before that wind blows you away," Mickland offers and steps back to allow a scarred woman into the all-male gathering. Celia, the healer and political leader of the settlement of Serran, enters wearing a long black garment that had started its existence as quilted bedcovering. No one gives her a second look but the woman behind her strikes fears into some hearts.

"Nasserila, you have returned!" Hadrian announces. "You must save us."

"No, this is her sister," Celia answers. "I call her Farren for she knows magical things."

"What is your business here?" Mickland asks.

"I came to introduce my new friend, Farren, and to warn you that this house is the next target to the Valen," Celia states.

"I have nought here but paints and pictures. There is nothing they want." Mickland frowns.

"You are respected, with such support, you have the ability to topple their pretensions; they fear an organized attack against them," Farren tells him.

"More than half the population of this settlement are of Valen descent," Mickland answers. "There are but two non-Valen settlers with fighting experience, the rest are tradesmen or artists. I will not lead people into certain death."

"Even now when it is known that you are their next victim you will not step forward." Hadrian sighs.

"Perhaps you should lead this, Hadrian, as you are much to ready to urge others into a fight but I know you have little stomach for the task," Mickland tells him.

"You think I sit back and wait to die." Hadrian glares at Mickland.

"This is not a spat between you two. My brother and his family are dead and I have none to help me bury them. You are cowards, every one of you sitting here forever talking but never acting." The young man's hands curl into fists.

Hadrian looks at the young man. "Come Rabin, let us visit your brother's house and see if we can discern who attacked them and give your family a respectful funeral."

Hadrian glances around while he heads to the door with the young man. Most of the others follow giving time for much dust to blow into the building. The last man leaves just after the door is shut so even more dirt is blown into the house. Mickland goes to check his paints for damage.

"Do you think Hadrian will start a war with the Valen?" Farren asks.

"No one may tell for certain what another man will choose to do," Mickland answers,

"Should they be watched?" Farren asks.

Celia shakes her head. "I have a baby to deliver and you must not worry about these ones they talk yet refuse to act."

MICKLAND SECURES HIS HOUSE after his guests all leave. He cleans up the best he can before he starts to paint. Painting both thrills him and restores his composure. He will wait for people to return if they want to talk but he will not seek them out. He never asked that they come.

THREE DAYS LATER, none of the men had returned. His life settled into a pattern of eating and painting. He is in the middle of his project when a timid knocking came on the door. The quiet sound does not pierce his concentration and as time moves forward the knocks gets louder. Finally, he steps back to look at the whole picture and the knock finally gets past his mental concentration.

Mickland goes to the door and calls out before opening it. "Who is there?"

"Louren!" The voice comes back.

Mickland opens the door and quickly bring his neighbour's daughter inside.

"I have been knocking for a while. Did you not hear me?" She frowns and shivers.

"I was painting." He directs her to a seat by the fire and then hurries to make hot tea from herbs.

"Drink this, it will warm you up," Mickland tells her before sitting down on a nearby chair. "Then you can tell me why you have come."

Louren drinks the mixture and sighs. "I have come with strange news."

"Strange, how is it strange?" Mickland asks.

"I was to marry a young man, he wrote me this letter." She takes a page of paper out of pocket and hands it to him.

Dearest Louren,

I, with a group of others, have chosen to leave this settlement and create a new one in another place. I considered bringing you with me but then I realized just how dangerous this may become so I reconsidered and will return for you when I have a house built and the first crop harvested. With love, Rabin.

Mickland reads it twice. "You think he and a few others left?"

"I know for I have gone around the settlement to find who went with him. Only Valens and outcasts are left."

"It is dangerous for you to travel unaided." Mickland frowns. "Where is your father?"

"I do not know. He had an appointment with a member of Dion's family two days ago he left telling me that he would be back by evening. I was sick with worry about him when a child came to my door with that letter. My first thought was that it was some note from my father until I read it. Do I grieve for them or do I wait when there is little hope either will return?" She starts to rock back and forth. "How shall I survive alone?"

Mickland frowns. "Do you know who your father went to see?"

"Yes, Dion's son. I watched his house from a hidden spot all yesterday but there was no sign of my father." Louren shakes her head. "Why did Rabin go, do I not have grief enough?"

"Rabin grieves for his brother and family. He came a few days ago looking for help to bury them." Mickland frowns. "We must wait for I do not know which way they went."

"I will do nothing but cry if I return to my house." Louren says.

"You may stay but this one room is the extent of this place," Mickland tells her. "Once the spring comes perhaps you will have your answers about Rabin."

"If he is to build a house I must prepare my linens." Louren thinks aloud.

"Bring me news if you hear?" Mickland tells her.

A DOZEN DAYS LATER, Louren enters Mickland's home. "Mickland, quick, Alex and Bella have returned. They need help."

Mickland puts down his brush and follows her to where the two children were speaking with Celia and Farren.

"What is the news?" Mickland asks.

"It was a dragon," Bella says.

"A dragon has wings and can fly. This was just a large, fast beast," Alex corrects her.

"It runs fast enough to say it flew," Bella answers him. "It was red and its breath knocked Rabin over when he tried to fight it."

"It does not matter what you call it," Celia reproves them both. "Tell Mickland the rest."

"We heard crashing and then this dragon appeared. It was huge and we ran in the other direction with Hadrian leading the way. The dragon jumped us and ate him first. Then Rabin tried to fight it with only a large stick. The dragon breathed on him and he fell down. When the monster left as it came and Rabin revived. The next morning we had to run from the beast again and the person who ran the fastest was eaten." Bella frowns. "Rabin took us to the side and said put us behind a rock so we could sneak away and come for help. We slipped through rocks and came away. That was three days ago."

"How do we fight this dragon should it come here?" Mickland asks.

"We put together a rescue party so it does not come this far," Celia tells him. "And you shall lead it."

"What do you want me to do to it? Paint it?" he asks.

"Farren shall go with you," Celia tells him, "Along with anyone else you think will help."

Mickland shakes his head. "I am not Torg."

"If all it took was a Torg then I would send one," Celia answers. "Your friend Hadrian is dead, you must avenge him since he had no family."

"I told him not to go." Mickland frowns but Celia expression does not change. "I must get some supplies. I will be ready to go by tomorrow morning."

Celia nods and leaves. Farren does not follow her but walks alongside Mickland. She watches him coil rope and get a bag of food ready. He lays out the warmest clothes he owns.

"I will meet you at the east edge of the settlement in the morning. Louren, I must say good-bye to Louren." Mickland addresses his last comment more to himself than Farren.

"Who else will you take? What weapons do you have?" Farren asks.

"I have no weapons." Mickland frowns at her. "I am a painter. My training is in painting portraits of nobles."

Farren frowns. "Then I will invite a few people to come along." She leaves him to his preparations.

THE NEXT MORNING Farren is waiting with two Valen and two women. Mickland knew the women be Torg. They had guarded Princess Ishtar who vanished the day she set foot on Serran. The only one who follows Mickland is Louren.

"If I am to lead this rescue mission, then I need to know where we are going. Did Alex or Bella mark a trail?" Mickland asks Farren.

"I know which direction they travelled." Farren starts walking.

"You need to tell me." Mickland frowns as he tries to keep her pace.

"I will show you," Farren answers. "More lives will be lost if we tarry longer."

The Valen follow but those who are not Valen walk behind these men fearing an unprovoked attack.

Farren keeps a steady pace, which is faster than the rest of the party. She continues on past the time that Mickland would have called breaks for lunch and supper. By the time night falls even the Valen are struggling to put one foot in front of the other. Farren finally stops when it gets too dark to avoid walking into large stones.

Louren requires the support of the Torg to reach the place where Farren has stopped. Mickland frowns but he lacks the breath to argue about her pace.

The Valen make a fire and sit isolated from the rest. Farren does not sit but stands at a distance listening as it the night was whispering its secrets.

Mickland and the Torg sit around Louren. "I should not have come," Louren tells Mickland. "I am slowing everyone down."

"It is too dark to continue," one of the Torg tells her. "We should have rested and eaten hours ago."

Mickland frowns. "We should not have come. This is madness trekking uphill and downhill through these rocks looking for a monster."

Louren shakes her head. "I must see if Rabin lives."

The night is far colder outside their sturdy home and the wind blows around the rocks that they curl up to for protection. No one suggests the Valen share their fire.

THE FIRST MORNING LIGHT they are shocked to find people crawling amongst the rocks trying to keep themselves hidden from an overhead view. Mickland recognizes many of the men, who used come to his house, with their children and wives slinking through past him as he huddled against the cold.

"Where are you going?" One of the Torg asks one of the men.

"Back to the settlement, we cannot fight this dragon alone," he whispers. "Do not speak so loud that beast will hear you. We were wrong to leave the settlement. Nasserila's law warned us but we were desperate."

Soon all the men gather around Mickland as they tell details about the dragon. The whispers get louder as they tell of everything they had tried but which had not worked. The Valen take out paper to write down the stories but no one pays any attention to Farren. Even Louren once she spots Rabin is no longer thinking about the danger as the two young people reunite.

It was only as a large animal crashes through the rocks toward them that they all stop talking and stare at the beast that runs on its back feet with long strides. When discussion starts again, the men talk about how to fight the dragon and which methods had not worked the previous times it had appeared.

As the animal gets closer the discussion speeds up but no one is standing up or reaching for a weapon. The Torg women who have the most experience with fighting shake their heads at the idea of attacking such a large being with the weapons they carry.

The dragon is right on top of them before Farren springs to her feet and starts running. Her action brings gasps from those who had watched Hadrian and the other man eaten. The woman although small is fleet of foot as she runs away from the group. The beast is close on her trail as the ground grows steeper as she heads up the mountain side. Farren runs towards a slope with large stones that get smaller the higher she goes. The dragon at first just bats the stones out of the way causing an avalanche below but then the rocks grow smaller it starts having problems as stones slide out from under its feet. Farren is still running and the beast blows its noxious breath at her back but she is always a little too far away for the stench to be effective. Then in one second the beast is no longer following as every rock around it is sliding down the mountain side. Those people on the ground grab their family members and move back from the shower of rocks and dust that rise from where the great dragon now lies being crushed to death by the rocks it dislodged coming down from the mountain. At the sound, Farren stops and looks down.

Farren makes her way around the debris pile to avoid adding to it. Once she arrives, Fareen orders everyone to return to the settlement. The Valen turn and go with noticing the others actions. Those who had left the settlement gather whatever they still had to carry it with them. Mickland stares at the dragon as its icy blood coats and breaks the rocks on which it lies. His eyes roam over every detail.

"It is not safe outside the place the Narath gave you to live,"

Farren tells him.

"I want to remember the details so that I can paint it. Your victory needs to be remembered and when Valen write history they are not always accurate." Mickland finally nods and heads back the way they came the day before. "But I was also right. I have no ability to fight dragons." A shiver runs over him.

CELIA WAITS ON THEM to return. She asks questions and nods at the answers. "I no longer want to rule because I need to use my healing power for everyone's good. I appoint Farren, for she won the day and no one else."

"She did not use magic," one of the Valens says. "We watched."

"No, she used the laws of nature," Mickland says.

"Then she will no longer be Farren, the witch, instead she will rule as Warra, the law giver," Celia announces, "The truth about her shall be honoured."

Spike
Tracey Bentley

SPIKE WOKE UP NICE AND EARLY, rubbed his eyes then sat bolt upright. This was it, January 5th, his first day at proper school! Spike was the youngest son of Gruff and Samhera Scorchius. He had two older brothers and a very big sister call Vesuvius but he just called her Suvy, it was just easier.

He came down to the breakfast table and saw his mum had prepared eggs for Fergus and Fantail. Suvy had already eaten and left for work.

"Can I have giant's porridge please mum" said Spike "I've got to stay strong for school!"

Fergus and Fantail laughed so hard at their baby brother a little smoke came out.

"Of course dear, good choice" said his mum as she shot a scolding look over at the twins.

The brothers were only two years older than Spike but they had blown smoke since they were babies, far younger than Spike was now. The Scorchius family were North Atlantic Emerald Back dragons. They could trace their origins back to just after the Ice Age and were distant relations of the Loch Ness Monster. Nessie had chosen to live in the water but the Emerald Backs stayed on the land helping to form the land with volcanic eruptions and molten rock rivers. This was a strong heritage indeed and the importance was not lost on Spike, he just hoped he would learn how to breathe fire and smoke at school.

The twins teased him mercilessly about lacking in the flame department.

"You're a dud, Spikey boy," Fergus would say.

"I think he's adopted, Fantail. What do you think?"

"I'm not I'm not!" protested Spike.

"My markings are the same as Suvy's. Maybe you two are

31

adopted".

"We look like Dad. We have his tail and wing shape."

Spike never won against the boys and however mad he got with his brothers he never even blew out a tiny puff of smoke. He looked at his reflection in the pool outside his cave. His scales gleamed beautiful iridescent green that immediately distinguished him from the Hungarian Forest dragons and the Russian Mosshills. Spike knew he belonged with his family but he couldn't help feeling a little inadequate. Both his parents and Suvy reassured him constantly but Spike had to believe it on the inside.

Mum served a huge plate of porridge and placed it in front of Spike.

"I can't eat all this, Mum," said Spike

"Do your best, son. You need to be a strong dragon today," Mum replied calmly as she stroked his small neatly folded wings.

As she smiled down at her baby boy it was hard to imagine that Samhera had terrorised three whole cities for a decade. Then the miracle happened, she was tamed by the love of Gruff Scorchius. He was mean on the outside but a pussycat inside. As Nana Fury used to say his fire was only nostril deep. He was all sunshine and rose petals deep down. After a whirlwind romance, they tied the knot under a blood moon and not long after Vesuvius was on the way. Four baby dragon flints later and she was the perfect house dragon, adoring wife and mother. She still had that temper, boy did she, but she kept it in check these days.

As the boys were finishing their meals Dad walked into the dining cave.

"Ready for your first day, Spike," he enquired.

Spike nodded vigorously, his mouth full of porridge.

"Now, boys," Gruff turned to look at the twins with a stern look on his face.

"You look out for your little brother today. The older flints might try to pick on him, especially as he's a Scorchius. If that happens you need to tell me and I'll visit school tomorrow. Remember, if you don't do what I'm asking of you you'll have your Mum to answer to."

The boys nodded almost as much as Spike. Dad's fire was nostril deep but Mum's went right to her tail!! As Samhera placed her husband's breakfast on the table she looked at the boys and did a little smoke puff to display her agreement with her husband. Fergus and Fantail sat up straight and folded in their wings in submission. With that Samhera turned and continued to prepare the packed lunches for school. She secretly smiled as she packed three, not two as before. She secured the packages and then marked them with her signature scorch so her boys remembered how much she loved them.

One by one Fergus and Fantail collected their back packs that fit snugly just under their wing tips. Spike tried to put on the last pack and found it so big it sat on the base of his tail. His dad quickly came to the rescue, tightening the straps so he looked just the same as his older brothers.

The three boys went outside just as the dragon bus was arriving. It was actually a huge African Smoothsand dragon called Bert who took all the children to school but he liked being called the bus. Contrary to popular belief some dragon breeds are quite placid. An African Sander could blow a huge smoke and fire plume but they rarely fired up in anger, usually excitement or strangely, grief. Bert smiled at the Scorchius boys.

"Hello, little man, you must be Spike," Bert said as he helped the young dragon to his seat. Spike just beamed back at him. He was just so excited that he would finally be taught how to 'fire up'. He would finally feel like a real dragon.

The boys always enjoyed the ride to school. It looked even more spectacular in the winter semester because of the snow on the ground lying next to frozen streams. Bert was huge and could carry about twenty young dragons. Sometimes he did an extra swoop down and all his passengers give a little scream and sometimes a little smoke trail. Fergus and Fantail were busy talking to their classmates but Spike was just looking around in awe of all he could see. The world was even more beautiful today than normal.

"Err 'scuse me, is it your first day too?"

Spike turned round to see a Pink Spikescale sitting behind him. These dragons came from Polynesia and were such a beautiful colour. Apparently their unique colour came from eating exotic birds and flowers. The Imperial School of Prehistoric Dragons was certainly world renowned and welcomed the most promising young flints from everywhere.

"Yes, it is my name is Spike," He held out a small scaly paw to shake, as was the polite thing to do when greeting a lady.

"I'm Kauwela," she blushed a little when she took his paw. Spike just beamed again. He had a friend and they weren't even at school.

Fantail noticed this little introduction but decided not to say anything. If he was honest Fergus usually started the teasing of Spike and he just went along with it. He was younger by four whole minutes and quite a lot smaller than Fergus. As Bert rounded the final corner the glowing towers of The Imperial came into view. It was certainly an impressive building with its huge purple towers and turrets at both ends. In olden days, this is where the senior students practised guarding a princess but those days were long behind them now. They were there purely for decoration or the occasional display.

Bert came to a stop outside the school and all the students slid down his tail and on to the cobbled driveway.

"Bye, kids," Bert shouted as he flew off on his next pick up.

Spike was mesmerised by the mass of colour in front of him. Red Welsh, Black Mongolian, Blue Rubbletails, Yellow Leatherwings were just a few of the breeds that Spike recognised. He even saw a purple dragon. Now they were the stuff of legend and apparently came into being after a big party to model the Grand Canyon: where ever that was!

Students of all ages were gathering and moving towards their year signs. Fergus and Fantail made their way to the year three sign but not before pointing out to Spike and Kauwela where their line was. Spike noticed Kauwela didn't have a back pack on.

"Did you bring any lunch with you?" he whispered as they began to move into their line.

"I didn't know you had to," replied Kauwela looking disappointed.

"Don't worry we can share mine. Mum has put a huge err something in there we'll be fine."

"Thank you Spike. I-"

Kauwela was cut short by the teacher clearing her throat and sending out a smoke trail with a little flame to follow.

"Pay attention, please. I am your teacher for today. My name is Miss Colere," She was a Welsh Red, known for their intelligence and short temper. The class followed behind their teacher in silence, they were new after all. Spike couldn't help admiring the vivid red of Miss Colere's folded wings as the sun caught them on the tip. She was a tall and slender dragon but you could tell she had a formidable wing span and a very athletic physique. Welsh Red dragons were no push over and Miss Colere certainly meant business.

As the young dragons filed into the classroom there was an air of excitement. The walls were adorned by posters of the most feared dragons in history with their biographies next to them. Spike saw both his mum and dad on the wall but kept quiet. On the blackboard were the most exciting words ever.

BREATHING FIRE: LESSON 1

Miss Colere began with instructing the students about general safety and rules within the school, what they had to remember and their locker numbers. Spike was totally oblivious; he just stared at the blackboard imagining the instructions to help him breathe fire magically appearing.

"Spike. Spike!!"

Miss Colere had noticed who wasn't paying attention and wasn't happy.

"Where were you young man because you certainly weren't listening to me!"

"II..ww was..dddrreaming of breathing fire ...mmmiss," he stammered

"These are very important rules, Spike. Do you think you don't need to know them? I understand you're a Scorchius but that's no reason to daydream."

A slight murmur went round the class. Damn it! Spike was hoping to stay anonymous with his classmates. Now everyone would expect him to be a flamethrower. This was too much pressure for the little green dragon. He imagined all the teasing when he failed and the disappointment but funnily enough he was more concerned that Kauwela wouldn't like him anymore. He felt even worse now. He looked over at her and she gave him a reassuring look, maybe he'd be ok.

After some theory about the art of fire breathing, Miss Colere showed a film of a dragon breathing fire, smoke, sparks, and the works. The whole class stared in awe as Spike just watched and felt a little nauseous. To everybody else they were watching Vesuvius the Great and Powerful, current holder of the Dragon Challenge Cup, Spike just saw Suvy his big sister. Spike hoped Miss Colere would use her official title and not her last name now that would be just too cruel. Maybe the dragons in his class were too young to put two and two together and realise why they knew the Scorchius name.

"OK class, it's time to start our practical fire breathing tutorial, let me just open the windows and put the fans on." Miss Colere busied herself preparing as she spoke.

She chose to go in alphabetical order of the register; Spike breathed a sigh of relief.

"Scale Atticus first."

A Roman Granite Tail stepped forward. They were a

distant descendant like the Emeralds. He shook his head, thrashed his heavy tail, flapped a little wing and blew a small pink flame.

"Very good, Scale," Miss Colere said encouragingly. "Now you will have more power if you flap your wings first before tail"

"OK, Miss."

Shake. Flap. Thrash. The flame was bigger this time and redder. Scale walked back to his seat as the other dragons flapped their wings in applause.

One by one the little dragons were asked to come forward by their teacher and apart from the twin Antarctic Silverwings they all managed some kind of flame. The twins did give a strong smoke plume as they were notoriously poor with fire due to their cold habitat. Everyone still flapped to show support. Kauwela's flame was delicate and lilac but she maintained it for the longest time. Miss Colere was suitably impressed.

Now it was Spike's turn. He tried to remember all the tips that the teacher had given the other students as he took his position. Shake his head, wiggle his ears (a signature Scorchius move), flap his wings, thrash the tail- Blow!! Nothing. Nothing at all. Spike just looked sadly at Miss Colere who was in shock.

"Try again, Spike," she urged.

Spike went through the same ritual for the same result. Even when Miss Colere changed it up a little the result was the same. The last time he tried the teacher watched intently. She then came to Spike and felt above his snout and under his jaw.

"Spike, I think you should see the nurse. I'll take you."

As the class waited for an assistant to watch over them they all whispered and wondered what was wrong with Spike Scorchius. Spike just stood there not knowing what to think or do. The assistant arrived and Spike and Miss Colere walked to the nurse in silence. When they got there the classroom events were reported to the nurse along with the snout-checking exercise. The nurse just stared at Spike and muttering to herself did the same checks again.

"Ok, young dragon, you need to be brave for me, this will probably sting and maybe hurt a little," said the nurse in a calm and reassuring tone. Even though she was a Greenland Blackheart Spike did feel a little less scared. He still tried to sink into the hard plastic chair he was sitting on though.

"Now follow my instructions carefully, however silly you feel."

Spike nodded

"Stand up and thrash your tail, all the time trying to blow fire, then stand on your head"

Spike complied without question although he did think how silly this must look, a little green dragon stood on his head while a red and black dragon were watching.

"Now wiggle your ears and try to blow. If you can do it while standing on your head all the better"

Miss Colere steadied Spike so he didn't fall over while wiggling and blowing! After all these antics the nurse felt his snout then brought a huge pair of fire pliers. Spike gulped as the nurse stuffed the pliers up his snout. Boy did she wriggle them around it stung a lot, and hurt a lot too.

"There!" she announced triumphantly as she pulled out a small bone person from Spike's left nostril. Spike recognised the piece from one of Fergus's play village toy sets. Although his snout was really sore Spike felt strangely better. The nurse then bathed his snout in warm water and put balm just on the inside edge.

"Now do not try to blow until after lunch," the nurse instructed.

"Don't worry Spike will stay with me today," said Miss Colere as she put a paw on his wings.

Spike sat at the back of the class for the rest of the morning lessons but he knew everybody was looking at him. When the students were dismissed for lunch Spike didn't move, Kauwela went to the teacher.

"Miss Colere, can I stay too please? Spike and I are sharing lunch today."

"Of course, that would be a lovely thing to do. I'm sure Spike would prefer that. I will stay here as I can't leave you alone but I'll have some drinks brought in."

Spike and Kauwela shared lunch as Miss Colere sat at her desk checking books and writing a letter to Spike's parents. They all had big glasses of lavaberry juice, a great treat for these little dragons. Spike was right; his mum had packed enough food for at least three dragons!

Meanwhile Fergus and Fantail looked for their little brother in the playground. They couldn't see him anywhere so they grabbed the Antarctic Silverwings and demanded to know where Spike was.

"He's had to stay behind in ccclass," they stammered "And he had to go to the n.n. nurse."

Oh no, Mum would kill them or at least give them a good scorching! They went to the classroom and saw Spike and Kauwela laughing and talking as they ate. The twins rushed in.

"Spike, are you okay, little brother? We've heard you had to go to the nurse!"

"I'm fine, I think," replied Spike. "Oh and I've got your little bone person you lost from your play set. It was in my snout, can you believe it?"

The boys flashed a look between them that said they had known where the missing piece was all along. Oh dear, they were really in trouble.

After lunch, Miss Colere invited Spike to try and breathe fire once again. He stood at the front of the class shook his head, wiggled the ears, flapped the wings, thrashed the tail and blew. A tiny orange flame escaped from both nostrils steadily growing in strength. Spike was breathing fire!! The little dragon felt ten feet tall. The rest of the class flapped their wings in celebration. Kauwela was flapping so hard she nearly lifted off her seat, Spike felt himself blush. A little smoke came out.

ON THE RIDE HOME the two young dragons blew smoke nearly all the way. Fire wasn't allowed on Bert's bus but Spike didn't care, he couldn't even blow smoke this morning. Miss Colere was so clever to spot the problem. By the end of the journey, Spike blew a smoke heart for Kauwela, now it was her turn to blush.

At the dinner table, Mum and Dad read the letter from Miss Colere and were mortified.

"We're so sorry, Spike, we had no idea," said Mum in a quivering tone.

"It's okay, Mum," said Spike "I'm just glad Miss Colere is so clever."

Mum turned her attention to the twins and there was no quiver in her voice this time.

"And what do you two know about this mysterious vanishing toy?"

The boys just stared and stammered

"I must have done it, Mum," said Spike "I was always fascinated with those toys."

"All right, son, as long as you're better now," said Mum tickling Spike's ears, he loved that.

The twins relaxed. They had dodged a scorching thanks to their little brother; they made a silent promise to treat him better in future.

That night the Scorchius family were entertained and warmed by the fire breathing antics of Spike. Even Suvy was impressed so he blew her a little smoke heart. He finally belonged; he was a real North Atlantic Emerald Back dragon!

About the Authors

SARAH DAHLMANN is a mother and owner of Howling Wolf Books. She is also a writer as well as a designer and crafter with big dreams.

JENNIE EVANS is a Kelowna-born writer and artist. When she's not drawing weird and wonderful fantasy creatures, she can be found passionately ranting about wildlife and plants to anyone who will listen. Her favourite animals are crows and ravens.

FRANCES G. MANTLER is a wife and mother of three. She likes to spend her time gardening. The Magic of Serran is the first novel she wrote, which was published at the insistence of her children who read it long before it took its final form.

TRACEY BENTLEY is 49-years-old and originally come from Salford, just outside Manchester, England. After successful careers in international banking and ballroom dancing, she has returned to her childhood passion, storytelling. She is honing her passion by studying creative writing at Okanagan College and living in "Beautiful British Columbia" with her partner and two greyhounds.

B. HEATHER MANTLER is a lover of fairy tales and fables. Her home town is Prince George, British Columbia. Heather is always working on another story as she hopes to finish every story idea that she has ever written down. Her blog is heathersdomain.wordpress.com.